DID YOU SWIM TODAY, OLIVER OTTER?

For Annie
With Thanks to Loudwater

First published in Great Britain in 1996 by Sapling, an imprint of
Boxtree Limited, Broadwall House, 21 Broadwall, London SE1 9PL.

10 9 8 7 6 5 4 3 2 1

ISBN: 0 7522 0696 6

Origination by Loudwater
Printed and bound in Italy by L.E.G.O
A CIP catalogue entry is available from the British Library.

DID YOU SWIM TODAY, OLIVER OTTER?

KATE VEALE

🌿 *sapling*

Oliver Otter lived near the river at Sandy Hole.
Every evening he put on his shiny red boots
before climbing into the bath.
"Why do you put your boots on, Oliver?"
his mother would ask.
"Because I don't like getting my feet wet."
"Oh dear," she would sigh. "How will you
ever learn to swim?"

One night, Oliver's mother tucked him into bed and said, "Sleep well, little one. Tomorrow we'll go down to the river."

Oliver woke early because he was so excited.
"What's the river like?" he called out.
"Follow us, and you will see," laughed his
mum and dad.

They led the way out of dim
Sandy Hole into the bright sunlight.
There were lots of smells today,
particularly from the cows
in the nearby field.

They ran down to the river bank.
"I'll go in first," said his dad,
"and you can jump in after me."
"I'm not going in there, Mum," gulped Oliver.

"It's too deep for my boots!"

His mum hugged him. "We can swim
in together," she said.
But as soon as they were in the water,
Oliver climbed on to her head.
 "I don't want to get my feet
wet," wailed Oliver.
 "Oh dear," sighed his mother.
"What ever shall we do?"

DON'T
STOP 'TIL
YOU GET
TO THE
SHOP.

So out they climbed on to
the river bank and set off
to the local shops.
  "We'll find something to help
you like the water," said his dad.

At the shop, Oliver chose a big yellow rubber ring with a duckling's head and tail and orange feet, a yellow fishing net, and some blue plastic sandals. Back they went to the river to try again.

New blue plastic shoes

LUCKY DUCKLING

Nets for catching things

"Watch me!" said Oliver's dad.

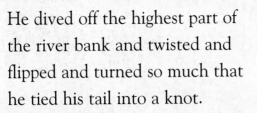

He dived off the highest part of
the river bank and twisted and
flipped and turned so much that
he tied his tail into a knot.

"That is daddy's prize winning slip-knot dive.
Would you like to have a go?"

"Not likely," said Oliver, thinking of how wet
his feet would get.

Instead he put the rubber ring
into the river and sat on it,
and keeping his feet well out of
the water, he paddled quickly
up the river.

"That's not swimming, that's canoeing!" laughed
Oliver's mum, and they all went home to tea.

The next day, Oliver woke even earlier.
He put on his blue plastic sandals,
picked up Lucky duckling, the net
and a jam jar and tip-toed out of Sandy
Hole to go down to the river by himself.

"Today I'll try getting my feet a little bit wet!"
thought Oliver.

He ran down the bank to the river and paddled
carefully through the shallows fishing around
in the weed with his new net. All of a sudden,
a slimy creature stuck its head out of the net
giving Oliver a fright.

"Aaargh!" shouted Oliver. "It's a dinosaur."

"No, I'm not a dinosaur. I'm
a newt and my name is
Trevelyan," said the
newt proudly.

"Oh good!" said Oliver (he knew that
dinosaur's could be dangerous). Then he
added "My name's Oliver Otter and I have to
go home now. Would you like to come too?"
"Yes, please," said Trevelyan.
Oliver put him into the jam jar so that
Trevelyan could poke his head out and
talk as they went along.

On the way home, Oliver asked if Trevelyan
liked swimming.

"I love it," said Trevelyan. "And I love the river.
We can play there every day."

They arrived at Sandy Hole just as Olivers'
parents were getting up.

Oliver only had time to put Trevelyan under
the bed and pull the covers over himself before
his mother came into the room.

"Aaargh," she said, horrified, when she saw
Trevelyan. "It's a dinosaur."

"No," said Oliver, proudly, "it's a newt.
He's called Trevelyan, and he's my friend.
He's going to help me learn to swim."

Every day after that, Oliver stuck his head
out of Sandy Hole, sniffed the air and ran
down the hill with Trevelyan to the river.

FISH
SWEET
FISH

Every evening when they got home Oliver's
mum and dad asked: "Did you swim today?"

I'm already dead

"No, Oliver would reply: "but I caught a fish,"
or
"No, but Trevelyan nearly got eaten by a duck,"
or
"No, but we found a frog."

Then one day, when Oliver stuck his head out
of the tunnel and sniffed, a cold white flake got
up his nose. He sneezed. Instead of being green
the fields were white.

"It's snow," exclaimed Trevelyan, "and my tail
has frozen."

Oliver got a hot-water bottle,
half filled it with water and
put Trevelyan in it so that
his tail could warm up.
Soon he felt warmer.
"Let's go sledging!"
suggested Trevelyan.
"Don't go too fast!"
warned Oliver's mum.

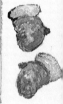

The cow is in a
nice warm barn.

They fetched Lucky duckling to use as a sledge
and Oliver held on to the neck. Trevelyan
grasped Oliver's hat, they tied the hot-water
bottle to Lucky duckling's tail, and off they went.
The hill from Sandy Hole to the river was very
steep and the Lucky duckling sledge went faster
and faster, FASTER and FASTER, FASTER -

- FASTER AND FASTER until -

SPLASH! they went over the river bank with a double somersault and into the river. Oliver laughed and swam to the shore. Trevelyan was speechless with surprise.

"You swam!" said Trevelyan.

"Did I?" said Oliver, amazed.

"Yes," - and Trevelyan danced a little celebration jig.

They sledged all day until the evening and when they went home, Oliver's mum and dad asked:

"Did you swim today?"

'Well done Oliver!'

"Yes," said Oliver, "and it was so cold I'm really looking forward to a deep warm bath with lots of bubbles - because I *love* getting wet!"

THE END